"When it comes to my work,
I will give you nothing before I give 99%."
— V.T.

"In loving memory of my titi, Maria Nichols and my
abuelo, Dr. Adolfo Latorre."
— A.L.

Acknowledgments

Thank you, Monica Isom, Dwayne Kohn, Lachandra Palmer, Janice Stewartson, and Tabitha Williams for taking time out of your busy schedules to read and critique *Cornbread* prior to publishing. The roundtable discussions we shared were hilarious as well as invaluable.

Has a Bad Habit

Vincent Taylor

Illustrated by Adolfo Latorre

Published by

TriEclipse Publishing
P.O. Box 7763
Jacksonville, FL 32238
www.trieclipse.com
904-778-0372

ISBN 13: 978-0-9704512-5-5
ISBN 10: 0-9704512-5-3

Published in the United States by TriEclipse Inc.

Library of Congress Control Number: 2006909501

Printed in the United States of America

Contents

The Cornbread Series by Vincent Taylor

Cornbread
Has a Bad Habit

Chapter 1

Roscoe's Dirty Little Trick

"Cornbread, I'm going over to get some chips. Are you coming?" Roscoe asked.

"No, because I know you don't have a penny to your name," I answered.

"What are you talking about? Seriously, let's get something to snack on. Chips, cookies, whatever. It doesn't matter to me. Let's just pick something up," he suggested.

Roscoe has this way of *going to pick something up*, but never spending his money.

We walked in and, of course, Roscoe saw everything he wanted. Well, so did I.

"Hey, I'm gonna have to **boycott** Mr. Lopez's store. His snacks are too doggone expensive. Look at this candy bar!" I complained.

"Gosh, will you stop being such a cheapskate, Cornbread? The candy only cost forty cents," Roscoe snapped back.

Roscoe strolled down every aisle with this silly grin on his face as if he was planning something.

"What are you up to, Roscoe?" I asked curiously.

"Nothing," he answered, throwing his palms up to me.

We stayed a little while longer. I glanced over from another aisle and saw him in the surveillance camera with a bunch of candy.

Mr. Lopez has these two cameras in the store so that he can catch anyone who is trying to steal.

Oh! And when he sees a bunch of kids outside his store, he instantly points to the sign he wrote with a black marker. "ONLY 2 STUDENTS AT A TIME."

I made my way over to the drinks where Roscoe

was standing.

"Where is it?" I asked angrily.

"Where is what?" Roscoe said innocently.

"You know, the candy," I responded.

"Hey, don't you worry about me. Do you have your money?" he asked with a grin on his face.

"You better not be doing what I think you're doing!" I said, getting worried.

"Yeah, yeah, yeah. You just make sure you have your money. And pull yourself together while you're at it. You look like you're about to have a nervous breakdown with your scary self."

I walked around a little while longer, and Roscoe was nowhere to be found.

After I picked out what I wanted, I went to the counter. Mr. Lopez rang up my bag of chips and a soda.

"That'll be four dollars, kid."

"FOUR DOLLARS! Mr. Lopez, now I know I might hold on to my money tightly sometimes. Okay, maybe I hold it like that all the time. But I

just don't see how this little bit of food costs four dollars."

He pointed to Roscoe who was now standing outside.

Roscoe was laughing his head off about something and constantly moving his mouth, saying the same thing over and over. It looked like he was saying "I got you, Cornbread."

"Your friend said you were going to pay for his food, too," Mr. Lopez responded.

I don't believe this. He tricked me and I ended up paying for everything. So from this day on, I won't ever buy anything unless Roscoe is at the counter with me.

We left the store and headed for home.

"We had better hurry up. It looks like it's about to rain cats and roosters," he said.

"Cats and roosters?" I repeated, letting out a laugh.

"Yeah, cats and roosters! Are you hard of hearing?"

After I almost passed out from laughing so hard, I said to myself, *please tell me my best friend is joking.*

"Don't you mean 'raining cats and dogs'?" I asked out loud.

"Cornbread, do you see Ms. Robinson here?" he asked with an attitude.

"No," I responded.

"Well then, stop trying to play teacher. I don't care if it's 'cats and dogs,' 'cats and hogs,' or 'cats and chicken claws.' You know what I mean."

"Roscoe, did you feel that?" I asked, looking towards the sky.

Before I could get another word out, Roscoe shot past me.

I thought we would make it before the rain really started coming down. But I was wrong.

By the time I got home, it felt like I had just jumped out, no better yet, jumped into the shower.

I finally reached the front porch, but I was soaked.

"Cornbread, what happened to you?" asked my sister with a stupid smirk on her face. "Looks like somebody had an accident in his pants. You couldn't make it to the bathroom, huh?" Tiffany laughed as she continued making fun of me.

I didn't pay the brat any attention. I just went to my room and started playing my favorite beat.

Chapter 2

Talking Back to the Teacher

Boom, tic, boom boom boom boom, tic, boom boom, tic.

"Man, that beat is hot, Cornbread!" Roscoe exclaimed as he paused from drawing a picture of a car with some smooth rims on it.

The rest of the class was jamming as I continued with the beat.

"Cornbread, could you play it again?" asked three students as I finished.

I got requests like this every day.

It didn't matter to me. I would beat on the dry-erase board, the cafeteria tables, anything, just as long as I could produce a fresh sound.

"Isaiah! Is that you again?" asked Ms. Robinson as she walked back into the classroom.

I don't know why she won't call me Cornbread like everyone else.

"Yeah," I said, knowing I was about to get chewed out.

"Yeah?" she looked down at me with her hands on her hips.

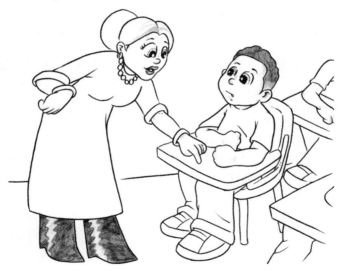

"I mean, yes, ma'am," I quickly responded.

"Does this desk look like a drum to you, young man?" she asked, though not expecting an answer.

"I have told you **numerous** times, Isaiah, that this is not your music class. You have a bad habit of beating on your desk when you know you're not supposed to.

"When you go to see Mr. Tolbert for music class, then you can beat, but not in here. So your parents can expect a phone call tonight since you can't seem to remember the classroom rules," she uttered.

"Maaaaan!" the entire class said in unison.

I was embarrassed. Every eye in the room was on me. I had never gotten into trouble like this before. Roscoe, on the other hand, well that's another story.

All of a sudden, this weird feeling came over me as everyone continued staring. Before I knew it, I had done it.

I said the one thing that teachers can't stand to hear. I didn't try to say it. It was like I had too much chapstick on my lips and it just slipped out.

"I don't care," I said in a low tone.

"What did you say, ISAIAH CARLTON WALKER?"

I was definitely in hot water. There was no turning back now or trying to apologize for the words I had let come out my mouth.

I was speechless. I couldn't say a word if my life depended on it.

With a surprised look in his eyes, Roscoe whispered, "Boy, you have truly … lost your mind!"

Ms. Robinson walked towards the front door, shaking her head, with a frown on her face.

"Isaiah, I need you to step out in the hallway for a minute," she said, biting her lips.

Just before I could reach the door, the alarm went off for a fire drill.

The class lined up like we had practiced many times before.

"Symone, don't forget to get Tiger," Ms. Robinson said as she exited with the rest of us.

"Yeah, we don't want to leave that goofy-looking goldfish behind," said Roscoe as he went out the back door.

Tiger is our fish that Symone volunteered to bring to school as our class pet.

Every other Friday, one of us gets an opportunity to take Tiger home so that we can take care of him.

"Aaah, man! Cornbread, after that comment, Ms. Robinson just might see me as a good kid now," Roscoe whispered as we continued walking.

While outside, I looked over and saw Tiffany in the line with the rest of her second grade class.

I just shook my head because I knew Tiffany would be by my class after school. She'd ask Ms. Robinson how I did in school so that she could tell Mom.

We entered the classroom and the first thing that came out of Ms. Robinson's mouth was, "Isaiah, LET'S GO!"

I was praying that it would slip her mind, but I should have known better.

"Is your mom home?" she asked.

"No. I mean no, ma'am," I replied in a hurry.

We were getting closer and closer to the principal's office. I swear I was about to faint.

"I'm sorry, Ms. Robinson," I said in a pitiful voice, hoping she would just turn around and give me another chance.

"I'm surprised at you, Isaiah," she said in a disappointed voice as we walked into the main office.

I really wasn't trying to be rude to her.

"I can't believe you would disrespect me like that. This is so unlike you. I don't …" she stopped in mid-sentence and just shook her head.

I didn't know what else to say. She was clearly hurt.

"What's your mother's work phone number?" she asked.

"Umm...3...7...8... um... I can't remember the rest," I said nervously.

"What do you mean you can't remember?"

"She just started a new job last week, and I don't know her number," I replied.

My left hand was shaking so much, it looked like it was sitting on top of a worn out washing machine.

I eventually put it in my pocket so she wouldn't see how I was trembling.

"Isaiah, you can definitely expect a phone call at your house tonight," she said as we walked back to the classroom.

Chapter 3

The Mystery Letter

"Isaiah! Isaiah!" yelled my father from the attic.

"Sir?" I responded slowly as I tried watching the last bit of wrestling on TV.

"Turn that television off and get up here so that you can help us with this ceiling," he shouted.

Mr. Williams and my dad were up there trying to fix it so rain wouldn't leak into the house anymore.

Dad jokes with Mr. Williams sometimes, calling him "Mr. Fix It," because he can pretty much fix any and everything in a house.

"Dad!" I hollered, "Can I finish looking at the last five minutes of wrestling?"

"Boy, you better get yourself up here right now! And bring a light bulb while you're at it," he hollered back.

As I carefully climbed the ladder with the light bulb in my hand, I could hear the TV when one of the wrestlers hit the hard canvas.

I hurried down the ladder just in time to see the referee pound on the mat to announce the winner.

"I'm coming, Dad. I had to um… go back and get the light bulb," I shouted, knowing good and well I was telling a fib.

Mom said I'm addicted to wrestling.

Huh, but I can stop if I really wanted to. I just don't want to.

I quickly climbed the ladder so he wouldn't have to call again.

"Aaah, man! It's dark up here," I said as I heard them talking *AGAIN* about starting their own business.

I couldn't see my hand in front of my face.

"It's about time you got here," Dad said.

"What's happening, lil' man?" asked Mr. Williams as he reached to give me a high-five.

Mr. Williams was *COOL!* It didn't matter what he said or what he did. He was just cool with it.

Boom, tic, boom boom boom boom, tic, boom boom, tic.

With my left hand, I began beating on the wood in the attic.

"Isaiah, I told you about all that fuss. Stop it and pass me the screwdriver. You know, if you studied as much as you beat on stuff, you would be a straight 'A' student," Dad said.

Mr. Williams was smiling and bobbing his head, though.

"That sounds pretty good," he said with a smile.

Ring, ring, ring. The telephone sounded.

"I'll get it, Dad," I said anxiously as I started towards the ladder.

"Boy, you better not go down there. Your sister can get it," he said without cracking a smile.

"Cornbread, it's Roscoe. He wants to know if you are still coming over to his house," Tiffany yelled.

"Tell him I'm busy, but he can come over here," I said while looking for Dad's approval.

"If he comes over here, he'll be right up in this attic working, too. So if you think he's ready to work, then sure, tell him he can come over. Otherwise, he needs to stay home," said Dad.

"Um…just tell him I'll see him tomorrow."

I know Roscoe like the **back of my hand** and trust me, he isn't going to want to work.

I remember one day Roscoe and I went to cut yards for some extra money. The only thing he did was carry the doggone gas can around.

I couldn't even get him to rake after I had finished cutting.

Well, anyway, finally Dad, Mr. Williams, and I fixed the leak in the attic.

I raced down the ladder before Dad found something else for me to do.

"So how was school today, Isaiah?" Mom asked as she sat at the dinner table with her shoes off.

Mom had recently started complaining about her feet aching. It's because she has to stand up all day at her new job at the bank.

"It was good," I answered. Then, changing the subject, I asked, "Do you want me to get the bucket of hot water today, Mom?"

Mom usually soaks her feet when she gets home from work.

"No, I'll be fine," she responded as she looked through the mail.

One piece looked strange. It did not have a stamp on it, and it looked like a kid wrote it.

Mom continued through the mail.

"What's this, Isaiah?" she asked, holding the

funny-looking letter up.

She turned it over and read the front. "TO MRS. WALKER, FRUM MS. ROBBERYSON."

"I don't know what it is, Mom," I said **nonchalantly**.

Mom opened the letter, began reading and started smiling. Quickly, that smile turned into a frown. Then she looked at me.

As she continued reading, her eyes stretched wide open. Her mouth dropped as if there were a ton of rocks in it.

She blew a quick breath out of her nose and glanced at me again.

This can't be good, I thought to myself.

"Isaiah, so I see you want to be grown. You want to talk back to Ms. Robinson, huh?" she said, squinting her eyes and blowing out another breath like a raging bull.

My heart speeded up, and I instantly started sweating. I just stood there shocked. My mouth was dry, and I was totally lost for words.

How can I put this? Mom doesn't play!

"Boy, go to your room! Also, you can forget about going to karate class, watching television, or anything else this week," she hollered.

As I got ready to close my room door, I saw Tiffany in her room with that silly grin on her face.

"What?" I hollered, but not loud enough for Mom to hear.

Tiffany didn't say a word.

"What?" I asked again.

"Guess what I wanna be when I grow up, Cornbread?" she asked.

"Who cares! Gosh! What?!"

"A MAILMAN WOMAN!" she replied as she laughed and quickly slammed her door.

I should have known she would find a way to tell Mom on me.

No more television. But worse than that, no more karate practice. And I was really getting the hang of all the new stances and techniques that Sensei Thompson had been teaching us.

Chapter 4

Carrot Drum Sticks

As I stretched across my bed, I heard Dad telling Mom that he would be back shortly.

He had to run across the street to Mr. Williams's house and take him some of the tools he had left in our attic.

"Isaiah, you and your sister come with me," said Mom. "I need to drive to the grocery store."

"I got the front seat!" I yelled as we raced for the car.

Mom glanced at me and said, "No, your sister is

sitting up here this time."

We usually take turns sitting in the front when we ride with Mom.

The only time she gets to sit up front all of the time is when it's me, her, and Dad.

Dad always says a gentleman gives up his seat to a young lady.

Young lady? I thought to myself. Huh, she's not a young lady. She's a trouble-making, tattle-taling second grader. That's what she is.

As we drove to the store, Tiffany pointed at a bunch of ugly cars and said they were mine.

One car was green, but it had so many rust spots, you could basically say it was brown.

Another one looked pretty good, but it didn't have a motor in it.

The third car was sitting on bricks with only one tire.

I wasn't in the mood for playing.

"Mom, could you tell Tiffany to leave me alone?"

She just stared at me in the rearview mirror and continued driving.

We arrived at the store.

"Get me one of those baskets, Isaiah," said Mom.

As I searched for a good shopping cart in the parking lot, Tiffany ran towards the door.

"Watch this, Mom," she said excitedly, holding an old piece of stick as if it were a magic wand.

"Abracadabra," she said, waving it at the door.

The door opened, and we entered the store. Mom gave us her usual speech.

"Don't come in here begging for anything, you

hear me? And don't go around touching everything, either."

We both nodded.

"Isaiah, you and your sister go and get me some carrots, while I pick up the rest of the food," she said as she headed down aisle three.

Mom was making some beef stew, and she needed carrots to finish it.

We both ran to the produce section seven aisles over.

"I'll pick them out, Tiffany. You just get the plastic bag to put them in."

I had to test the carrots to see if they were good, but I didn't taste them.

I had my own special way of making sure they were the best carrots for Mom's stew.

Boom, tic, boom boom boom boom, tic, boom boom, tic.

That was the sound of the carrots beating on top of the watermelons.

I knew I was taking a chance, but I kept on beating with my carrot drum sticks.

Just as I was finishing, I heard a voice behind me shout, "Hey, what do you think you're doing playing with this food, son? Who are you here with, anyway?"

"Our mom," Tiffany blurted out like he was talking to her. "If you want me to, I can go and get her. She's just on the other aisle."

Tiffany was trying her best to get me in trouble.

"I'm sorry, sir," I quickly apologized. "I won't play with the food again."

Just as the manager finished **reprimanding** me, I heard Mom approaching.

Boy, was I scared! I just knew he was going to tell on me, but he didn't say a word.

Of course, Tiffany had witnessed the WHOLE thing.

She began smiling. I knew what that meant.

"Cornbread, what do you think Mom would say if she found out you were using carrots as drum sticks?" she asked, holding out her hand.

I couldn't believe this! She was trying to blackmail me.

"Would you look at that!" she said with excitement, pointing to the candy section.

I knew where this was heading. Money out of my pocket.

"I sure would love to have a piece, NO, a pack of bubble gum, Cornbread," she said as Mom continued shopping.

I was at her mercy. There was nothing I could do at this point.

"Go ahead and get it," I said, counting the small amount of change in my pocket as I frowned.

As soon as we got back home, the phone rang. It was Ms. Robinson.

I heard Mom say, "Well, you can best believe he won't ever do that again."

"I was honestly shocked, Mrs. Walker. It isn't like Isaiah to talk back to a teacher," said Ms. Robinson.

"Like I said earlier, this will not happen again. Well, Ms. Robinson, you have a great night. And feel free to call me any time," Mom said.

Chapter 5

The Skating Field Trip

"Cornbread, you look like a big ol' bumble bee with that outfit on," Roscoe said as I walked into the classroom.

I had on my favorite yellow sweat suit.

"Very funny," I responded.

"Hey, I'm surprised your mom is letting you go skating after what happened yesterday," he said in amazement.

Ms. Robinson had planned our roller skating field trip two weeks before, and I brought my permission slip back a week ago.

I was sure Mom had just forgotten that it was today, because I knew very well that if she had remembered, I would be sitting in another teacher's class until they returned.

"I guess she forgot about it, but she did say I couldn't go to karate practice or any place else this week," I said.

He shook his head in disbelief.

"Roscoe, are you still going to the wrestling match this weekend?" I asked.

"No. You know my mom isn't gonna let me go if you're not going. So we better enjoy this skating while we can," Roscoe stated.

"Two in a seat," Ms. Robinson said as we boarded the bus. "I only want two students per seat."

Everyone was trying to push past someone so that they could sit by their best friend.

"And don't sit by anyone who's going to get you in trouble," she called out, looking directly at Roscoe and me.

Ms. Robinson had two chaperones to go on the trip with us. She made sure one of them sat in the back of the bus to keep an eye on us boys.

We were on our way to the skating rink. I couldn't wait to get there so I could see who was going to fall on their butt.

Field trips were fun. Even though Ms. Robinson was strict, she would let us sing songs on the bus as long as we didn't get too loud.

"Attention, attention, everyone!" said Symone as she snapped her fingers twice. "I need all eyes on me at this time. Allow your ears a chance to hear greatness as I sing this beautiful ballad for you all today," Symone said, clearing her throat.

"Cornbread, listen to Symone up there sounding like a sick chicken," Roscoe whispered as he jokingly covered his ears.

Symone didn't see him, and she probably could care less about what Roscoe said.

They are always fussing with each other about something.

"Cornbread! Why don't you put a beat to Symone's song," David requested.

Boom, tic, boom boom boom boom, tic, boom boom, tic was the beat I pounded on the back of his seat.

The class went crazy! It even looked like Ms. Robinson liked how it sounded. She looked back at us kids and just started smiling.

Again, I pounded *boom, tic, boom boom boom boom, tic, boom boom, tic*.

All the kids chanted, "GO! GO! GO!" as I kept the beat going.

Mrs. Price, our chaperone, even enjoyed the beat I made. Her head was bouncing back and forth to the sound.

"Alright, let's hold it down. You all are getting too loud," Ms. Robinson said from the first seat on the bus.

I really felt bad now.

I have a teacher who does all types of fun lessons in class with us. She takes us outside to eat with her during lunch sometimes, and she even allows us to sing and rap on the bus during field trips.

And what do I do? Talk back to her in front of the whole class.

As we headed off the bus, I looked out of my watery eyes into Ms. Robinson's.

I believe she could tell what I was thinking about, because as I passed her, she placed her hand on my head, winked at me and said, "It's okay, sweetie. Go on and have some fun."

"Come on, Cornbread, let's go to the video games," Roscoe insisted.

"Are you crazy? I'm getting ready to skate circles around you," I told him.

I started putting on my skates.

I looked over to my right and guess who I saw putting on hers? Ms. Robinson!

Oh! This is really going to be funny.

"What's taking you so long, Roscoe? Are you scared?" I teased him. "Come on."

"Just hold your horses," he responded, patting his hair in place. "I wanna look good for all the girls before I get on the floor."

I looked out and everyone was skating. So we went out, too.

"Whoa!" Roscoe shouted, losing his balance as soon as his wheels hit the glossy wooden floor.

I yelled over the blasting music, "It looks like you're walking a tightrope!"

He got a little further around the rink and then it happened.

BAM! His butt hit the floor like a sack of rocks.

Evidently, Symone saw the whole thing, because she rushed over to him like she was a paramedic.

She looked down and immediately asked, "Are you okay?"

Roscoe, surprised by her concern, said, "I'm alright."

"I wasn't talking about you, silly. I was worried about the floor because you TORE IT UP!"

Symone laughed and then rubbed the floor like it was a little baby.

While still lying on the floor, he just stared up at Symone and asked in a pitiful voice, "Does your family even like you?"

Symone continued laughing and just skated off.

I was tired after skating five laps around the rink, so I got something to drink.

As I stood in line waiting for my order, the beat from the DJ's booth was hypnotizing. Before I knew it, I was hitting on the glass counter with my favorite beat.

Boom, tic, boom boom boom boom, tic, boom boom, tic.

"Stop that! Does this here look like a drum set to you, son?" declared the old man behind the counter. "You kids today don't have respect for anything."

"Sorry, mister. The beat just hypno..."

"Yeah, yeah. Anyway, here's your drink."

"Thank you."

We finally left the skating rink.

I couldn't believe how good Ms. Robinson skated. I heard that Roscoe fell again and, of course, Symone was right there to give him a few more of her sarcastic remarks.

Well, this will probably be my most exciting day for a while.

Chapter 6

Grandma Comes for Dinner

Ding dong. The doorbell echoed through the house.

"Isaiah, go see if that's your grandma and granddad," said Dad as he continued looking through his *How to Become a Millionaire Over Night* magazine.

I walked over to the door and got on my tippy toes so I could see who was on the other side of the peephole.

"It's Grandma Vanna! She has presents, too!" I

announced excitedly.

I couldn't wait to open the front door.

"Hello, Grandma Vanna," I said as my arms flew apart to give her a big hug.

"Hi there, Cornbread. How's my favorite grandson doing?" she asked, squeezing my cheeks.

I quickly wiped the crumbs off my mouth, because I knew what she was about to ask next.

"And where is Grandma's suga'?" she asked, turning her cheek to me.

I gave her a kiss and immediately asked, "Do you got anything for me in one of those bags,

Grandma?"

"It's *do you have anything,* not *do you got anything*," Mom fussed. "And what kind of way is that to greet your grandma?"

I'm thinking to myself, *it's the smart way. I don't want Tiffany to get all the good gift*s.

Well, actually everything Grandma brings is good.

"How's my beautiful daughter doing?" Grandma asked, looking at Mom.

She started blushing like she was a kid again.

"I'm doing fine, Momma. Where's Daddy?" she asked.

"Oh, he couldn't make it over today. He had to do some work in the yard," she replied.

"On a Sunday?" Mom said, looking surprised.

"Yeah, you know your dad. He's a workaholic," she said, and they both laughed.

"Hello, Momma," Dad said, entering the room.

"Hey there, handsome," Grandma said with a gigantic smile.

She looked over towards Mom and said jokingly, "Alicia, you better be treating my son-in-law well."

"I do, with his aggravating self," Mom said as she playfully popped Dad on the back of his head.

A few hours had passed, and Mom and Grandma were getting dinner ready.

"Tiffany, what do you call yourself doing?" I asked.

"Cooking," she said, rolling her eyes at me.

"Cooking? Girl, you couldn't even boil an egg the right way," I responded.

"Isaiah, stop picking on your sister," Mom pleaded.

Grandma added, "Cornbread, one day your sister will grow up to be an excellent cook."

You should have seen Tiffany. She was soaking it all up like a sponge. I mean she actually believed Grandma.

"Go get your dad and tell him it's time to eat," Mom said to Tiffany and me.

We walked out of the kitchen, and guess who was sitting at the table?

"Roscoe, what are you doing here?" I asked.

"I saw Mr. Walker outside, and he told me Grandma Vanna was here. I knew what that meant.

GOOD OL' FASHIONED COOKING."

"She's not your grandma!" Tiffany shouted.

"It's okay, Tiffany," Grandma said. "Hi there, Roscoe."

"Hello, Grandma Vanna. It sure smells good in there. What are ya'll cooking, Courage Chicken?" Roscoe asked.

"It's Curry Chicken, with your greedy self," Tiffany snapped.

Everyone sat at the table. We all joined hands as Dad said the grace.

"Amen," we said in unison as he finished.

"Wow! This meatloaf is terrific!" Dad said, licking his lips.

"Thank you, dear." Grandma replied.

"Alicia, now I see where you get your good cooking from," Dad said, looking at Grandma.

It got real quiet for a minute as everyone continued eating.

Then out of nowhere, Roscoe asked my grandma something.

"Why do you call him Cornbread?" he asked, with a mouth full of food.

"Excuse me? What did you say, Roscoe?" Grandma asked.

"I said why are you the only adult that calls Isaiah by his nickname?" he repeated.

Grandma just smiled at him.

"What?" he asked while all eyes were on him.

"You mean Cornbread has never told you how he got his name?" she asked.

"No, ma'am."

"Well, when he was about four years old, he didn't particularly like everything on his dinner plate like he does now.

"One day, he had some rice, pork & beans, chicken and cornbread. He ate some of his food and then told his mom he was finished.

"Oh no! Isaiah, you need to eat everything on that plate" is what his mom said to him that day.

"Well, lil' smarty-pants took the bread to his mouth and within two minutes, said he was finished again.

"So we all got up from the dinner table, and I began helping his mother clean up the dining room. And what did I see underneath the table? Cornbread!" Grandma said.

"He was under the table?" Roscoe asked, looking puzzled.

"No! Sweetheart, the child threw his cornbread under the table. And ever since that day, I started calling him Cornbread."

Roscoe burst out laughing, along with everyone else.

"So *YOU'RE* the one who gave him his nickname," he stated in amazement.

"That's right. It was Grandma Vanna," she said.

Chapter 7

Only Girls Jump Rope

"When everyone finishes defining their science vocabulary words, we will go outside for awhile," Ms. Robinson announced.

I couldn't believe it. It was a Monday. A MONDAY! And she was taking us out.

All of us hurried to look up the words before she changed her mind.

"Okay, those of you who are finished can line up," she said after twenty minutes had passed.

I grabbed the basketball. Roscoe reached for the

football, and Symone brought the Hula Hoop.

"You can take everything out, but make sure it all goes by the fence. The only thing we need right now is a jump-rope," Ms. Robinson said.

"A jump-rope?" Roscoe repeated.

"Yes, a jump-rope."

Roscoe and I looked at each other, disappointed, because everybody knows only girls jump rope.

"I'm not playing this girlie sport," Roscoe said to me as he threw the football up in the air.

I guess Ms. Robinson heard him, because she immediately responded.

"First of all, Roscoe, there's no such thing as a *girlie sport*. There are plenty of guys who jump rope. As a matter of fact, I know of a young man who gets paid a lot of money to travel all over the world to do one thing. And guess what that is? JUMP ROPE," Ms. Robinson said, looking at the entire class.

Just as she finished talking about the man, she grabbed the rope and gave one end to Symone and the other end to Gwen.

"Okay, Roscoe, don't tell me you're going to let this old lady outdo you," Ms. Robinson joked.

I couldn't believe it. First, Ms. Robinson skated and now she was about to jump rope.

"Now, don't you all turn too fast. It has been a long time since these old knees have done this," she said.

Gwen and Symone began turning. Then they started singing those songs.

"OH NO!! I'm not jumping to any girlie songs. Now, I'll jump, but not to those songs," Roscoe said, watching Ms. Robinson.

They started turning faster, and the whole class joined in.

"15, 16, 17, 18!" they all shouted.

"I have never in my life seen a grown-up jump as good as Ms. Robinson," I said to Roscoe.

"Yeah, she did okay to be so old," Roscoe agreed.

She even had a dress on. I guess that's why she kept her hands tightly pressed to her thighs, so it wouldn't fly up in the air.

"Whew!" Ms. Robinson said as she finished. "Now that was a workout."

She stood there, bent over with one hand on her hip and the other on her knee, trying to catch her breath.

"Does anyone know what science term was just demonstrated?" she asked. "You all just looked the word up before coming outside."

"I know, Ms. Robinson," shouted Symone.

"Well, of course you do. You probably know what time I brushed my teeth and picked a booger out of my nose this morning," said Roscoe.

"Boy, it's a good thing Ms. Robinson didn't hear you. You better be quiet," I said.

"Gravity!" she shouted. "It's gravity, Ms.

Robinson."

"That's correct, sweetie," she replied. "Because every time I jumped up, it was the force of gravity that pulled me right back down."

Ms. Robinson went and sat under the oak tree to get some shade, while the girls began to jump rope first.

"Cornbread, do you all want to play a quick game?" Roscoe asked as he threw the football into the air.

"Okay, but we're not playing tackle," I responded.

"What's wrong, you scared?" he teased, flapping his arms like a chicken.

"Hey, just throw the ball!"

Roscoe played football for one of the neighborhood park teams last year. I think he said they were called the Lions. And he was the running back.

I heard they went the whole season **undefeated**. Carlos said that Roscoe was their star player, too. He also said Roscoe was given the nickname Truck, because he would just run right over players whenever he had the ball.

"Remember, Roscoe, no tackling," I shouted to them from the other end of the field.

"Okay, are you ready?" he yelled.

Roscoe and Brandon threw the ball off to Carlos and me.

The football looked like a doggone jet going through the air. I couldn't throw it that straight even if I had an NFL coach giving me private lessons.

Carlos caught the ball, and it almost knocked the breath out of his tiny body.

He only ran about four yards before pitching the ball to me. I guess he remembered Truck was on the other side.

I caught it and went straight for the sideline. Now, I wasn't scared at first. But Roscoe was running so fast towards me, I just knew he forgot about us playing two-hand touch.

"Go, Cornbread! *Tú lo puedes hacer*," hollered Symone like she really knew Spanish.

Carlos is the only person who can understand what she was really saying since he speaks it fluently.

I didn't know what in the world she had said, but

I kept running anyway. Then she said it again, but this time in English.

"Go, Cornbread! *You can do it.*"

Luckily, I got around Roscoe, but he was right on my heels. As I looked behind me, his eyes didn't look like they were seeing his best friend. I believe he saw the team that beat them in the championship game last year.

I faked right, but he didn't fall for it. His arms opened wide like an eagle's wings, while he continued making eye contact. And then, it happened.

Chapter 8

The Falling Pot of Boiling Water

"Isaiah, what's wrong?" Mom asked, looking concerned. "Why are you walking like that?"

"I was playing football, and Roscoe *CLAIMS* he didn't try to tackle me," I answered.

Sitting on the couch, Dad said, "Hey, are you my tough karate man or what? You'll be okay. Tackling is just part of the game, son."

"But we said we were going to play two-hand touch," I complained.

"Well, that's your best friend, so I'm sure it was

just an accident," Dad said.

Accident? Yeah, right! He knew exactly what he was doing.

Tiffany overheard us talking. And with a concerned look on her face, she ran into the garage. I was surprised to see her react like that. I guess she was just somewhat upset that I got hurt, which is hard to believe.

We heard a bunch of noise like something fell. I hoped she hadn't hurt herself.

The silver knob slowly began to turn as the door opened.

Tiffany stuck her head in and started smiling, but it wasn't a genuine smile. It was a sneaky one.

"Tiffany, what is that you have in your hands?" Dad asked, realizing that she was holding something behind her back.

She brought out a dusty pair of crutches that used to be Dad's from his karate days.

"Here you go, Cornbread-the-limp," she laughed

as she attempted to walk on the crutches that were about two feet taller than she was.

Dad and Mom both started laughing. It was sort of funny.

"Alright, both of you go and get started on your homework before it gets late. You have school tomorrow."

I grabbed my books and went to the dining room table. Tiffany prefers to do her homework on the floor.

Boom, tic, boom boom boom boom, tic, boom boom, tic.

I began beating on the table.

I went to get some cookies, and while I was up, I began beating on the stove.

Mom had some hot dogs cooking, and the water had just started boiling. I made sure I didn't burn myself.

So again, I began beating.

Boom, tic, boom boom boom boom, tic, boom boom, tic.

There was something about playing the beat on the metal stove that made it sound REAL good. I got so caught up in the moment that I forgot about everything. I closed my eyes and played what would be one of my best beats ever.

However, since my eyes were not open, I didn't realize that the pot of boiling water was vibrating with every beat I made.

"Cornbread, will you stop it? That's irritating!" Tiffany shouted from the floor.

I couldn't stop, though. The beat was a part of me now. So with the very next beat, the pot vibrated closer towards the edge of the stove. I couldn't tell because my eyes were still shut.

I hit the counter three or four more times with the same smooth beat, and the pot slid in the direction of where Tiffany was lying.

On the very next beat.

BAM!! The hot water fell to the floor. Tiffany screamed at the top of her lungs.

"AAAAH!!!" she hollered like she had been pierced by an arrow.

My eyes quickly opened.

"OH MY GOSH!" I shouted, afraid to look down on my left where Tiffany was.

My heart began racing, and it felt like I was about to have a heart attack.

I finally got up enough nerve to look on the side of the stove. Tiffany was still screaming, while her hands covered her face.

I just knew her face was scarred for life. Slowly, I removed her trembling hands from her cheeks.

I couldn't believe what I saw.

I let out a deep breath when I only witnessed tears running down Tiffany's face.

Mom rushed into the kitchen.

"What's going on in here? What's wrong with Tiffany? Is she alright?" Mom asked in a really panicky voice.

"Yes, ma'am," I answered.

"Isaiah, what happened?" she asked again.

I explained that I was beating on the stove, and the pot of water fell. Then I hesitated before saying, "And it almost got on Tiffany."

"Didn't I tell you to stop all of that beating?" she exclaimed. "I knew something like this would eventually happen."

As she continued fussing, she just broke down and started crying.

"It's okay, Mom. Please don't cry," I begged.

"I'm sorry. I promise I won't do it again."

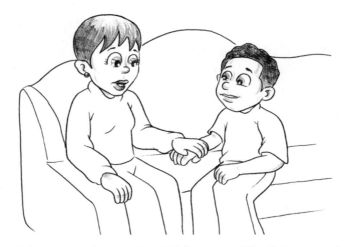

Mom saw how all of this was affecting me. So she sat me down and gently grabbed my hand.

"Isaiah, I don't care if you beat. As a matter of fact, I think you're an awesome drummer. You just have a bad habit of beating on things you shouldn't," she said calmly.

I listened attentively as each word came out of her mouth.

"You could have really injured your sister tonight," she continued. "I would have a nervous breakdown if anything ever happened to you or your sister."

"I'm really sorry, Mom. It's just, sometimes I don't even think about it and before I know it, I'm beating on things. But I promise, I won't do it again," I said with a tear falling down my cheek.

"Isaiah, I tell you what. If you can use enough self-control to stop all of that beating, I'll talk with your dad about possibly getting you a drum set," Mom said.

"ALRIGHT!" I smiled.

"Wait a minute. That includes using that same self-control when you're at school," she quickly said.

"Yes, ma'am. Mom, were you for real when you said that you really like my beats?" I asked.

"Hey, let's not miss my point. Yes, I think you play fantastic, but just try to remember when the right time and place to do it. You hear?"

"Yes, ma'am."

"Alright, go ahead and finish your homework."

Let me see. Ms. Robinson said we have to write a poem about our day and make sure that it rhymes.

A Day in Cornbread's Shoes

I limped from the tackle of Roscoe
Because in football he is like a pro.

I complained but Dad said 'be tough'
Because the game can sometimes be rough.

I have a sister who pulls no punches
Because when I limped, she laughed and brought
me crutches.

Boom, boom, tic is the sound I beat
Because I like to keep the kids dancing
on their feet.

Today my nerves were running raggedy
Because my habit almost caused a serious
tragedy.

Cornbread Breaks It Down

1. **Numerous** – Now that's when you're talking about a whole lot of something.

2. **Boycott** – Dad said it's when you've *had enough* and you refuse to buy or use a certain service from a company.

3. **Back of my hand** – That's one of those phrases Ms. Robinson taught us. She said it is called an *idiom*, but Roscoe keeps calling it an *idiot*. Anyway, she said it's when you REALLY know something without thinking twice.

4. **Nonchalant** – Whenever my dad wins a game of bowling, he never shows any excitement. That's a good example of someone being nonchalant.

5. **Undefeated** – I know this one! It's when you win every doggone game of something.

6. **Reprimand** – Oh! That's when your mom, dad, grandma, teacher or anyone is fussing at you.

About the Author

Vincent Taylor truly loves the pen. Starting with writing songs at a very young age, he has continued to cultivate his craft by branching out to write across various genres. As a result, he has published *Rhythmic Reading with Rap* (nonfiction), which was his first publication. *The Abstract Art of a Poet* is a book of poems that captured his poignant thoughts on society, family, and relationships. And finally, he has taken pleasure in penning the many books in the *Cornbread Series* (fiction).

Vincent travels the country, speaking to educators and students in the area of reading comprehension with his highly sought-after workshop entitled "Reading, Rappin' & Having Fun."

Mr. Taylor resides in Jacksonville, Florida, with his beautiful wife and two precious daughters.

Cornbread Class Set

* 12 books (Same Cornbread title)

* a CD-ROM filled with comprehension questions
  for ALL 8 chapters

* questions aligned with New Generation Sunshine
  State Standards, Georgia Standards and several
  other states' standards

* answer key for each worksheet

* blackline masters

Go to **www.CornbreadSeries.com** to order your
sets!

School Visits

Now that you've read my books, would you like for me to visit your school?

Go to **www.CornbreadSeries.com** to schedule your school visit today!

Also by Vincent Taylor

This workbook comes with a sing-a-long audio CD that teachers can utilize for enhancing vocabulary and comprehension skills such as main idea, context clues, topic and inference. This is an excellent resource to reach students who learn musically.

Order online at **www.TriEclipse.com**

School Visits

Reading, Rappin' & Having Fun
(Student Presentation)

Enjoy a fun-filled, educational presentation by author Vincent Taylor as he integrates hip-hop music and hand gestures to reinforce reading skills.

Reading performance standards such as *main idea, supporting details, topic sentences, context clues, and vocabulary* are addressed in this highly sought after, interactive presentation.

Mr. Taylor will totally engage your students by having them recite lyrics from their favorite song on the *Rhythmic Reading with Rap CD.*

Go to **www.VincentTaylor.net** to schedule your fun-filled school visit today!

Also, find out about *Reading, Rappin' & Having Fun* for teachers